RIDING THE ROCKET

- VOLUME ONE –

WESTBOUND TO KIPLING

Also by T. C. Downer

Open Prison
The Man in the Yellow Shirt
The Last Stop
Implied Emancipation
Speak English
The Forum
The Human Experience: A Collection of Short Stories,
Volume One

RIDING THE ROCKET

– VOLUME ONE –

WESTBOUND TO KIPLING

T. C. DOWNER

To my amazing parents, for always encouraging me to follow my dreams

CONTENTS

Kennedy / 9

Warden / 13

Victoria Park / 18

Main Street / 23

Woodbine / 27

Coxwell / 32

Greenwood / 37

Donlands / 42

Pape / 46

Chester / 51

Broadview / 55

Castle Frank / 60

Sherbourne / 65

Bloor-Yonge / 69

Bay / 73

St. George / 77

Kennedy

When my alarm clock sounded, I was already late for work. As I rose out of bed and headed into the bathroom, I was calm. I took my time in the shower, enjoying the water cascading on my skin. I took my time brushing my teeth, following it up with flossing and a rising with mouthwash.

I wasn't in a hurry, because I didn't care anymore. I was going to make my way to work, knowing full well that I would be written up for tardiness. Did I care? The answer to that is no.

For the last couple of months, I have been mulling over the same question, over and over again. Should I quit my job? The answer to that question was as complicated as it was easy.

I worked at a call centre located in downtown Toronto. I initially applied for the job as a means of temporary employment. Seven years later, the job didn't seem as temporary as it once did.

I hated my job. Everyone I interacted with on a daily basis was rude. The customers were rude. The managers were rude. My co-workers were rude. It's as if all the unpleasant people of the city just happened to migrate here.

As I took my time getting dressed, I thought about the way I would do it. I have been rehashing the same thing over and over again in my mind, for the last couple of days. When I went, they would all go too.

I slipped on my sneakers and knelt down to tie my laces. I applied foundation on my face, and some mascara around my eyes. I combed my hair, and let it fall delicately on my shoulders.

While glancing in the mirror, I whispered "Bye, so long" to my reflection, and left my rented basement apartment.

Walking towards the subway station, I contemplated turning back and going home. I contemplated just going back to sleep, and pretending that the thought never crossed my mind. But then I remember the reason why I was doing it. It had to be done.

I patted my pocket, making sure that I still had my special equipment; the equipment I would need to carry out the deed. Feeling it in my pocket, I continued my walk.

As I arrived at the subway station, I paid $3.00 for my fare. I had previously purchased a

Metropass for the month, but had given it away yesterday. I wouldn't need it where I would be going.

Going through the turnstile, another nagging thought popped into my head. *Give them another chance. Just try it. Come on.*

I couldn't get the voices to stop nagging me. They kept on talking and getting louder. The only way to get rid of them was to listen.

I could give them another chance. Maybe, just maybe, everything could go back to how it was before that place.

Give them another chance, I thought.

And so, I did.

Standing on the platform, waiting for the train to arrive, I spotted another woman. She was standing, as I was, waiting for the train.

"Excuse me, can you tell me the time?" I asked her.

I waited for an answer, but none came. She ignored me. Her rudeness pierced my heart like a million jagged daggers.

It was settled. There was no hope. There was no changing. Things had to unfold as they were meant to unfold.

The train pulled into the station. As I boarded

the train, I patted my pocket once again. They needed to learn. There was no other way.

Warden

"Hurry up, Jeremy! Go wake up your sister!" I yelled from the bottom of the stairs.

My son Jeremy and daughter Alia were very hard to wake up in the morning. We went through the same routine every day. And every day, we were always late.

"She won't wake up," my son said.

"Tell her I made pancakes."

"But she won't wake uh-uh-up." He pronounced *up* as if it were a three syllable word.

Resigned, I headed up the stairs straight to my daughter's room. She was the hardest one to wake up.

"Good morning, baby girl. It's time to wake up," I said gently.

She groaned and pulled the cover over her head.

"Please, can you wake up for daddy?" I pleaded.

"But, I'm so tired." She pronounced tired as *ti-erred*.

"I made pancakes for you. Blueberry with

strawberries on top."

At the mention of this, she jumped out of bed. I followed her into the bathroom, helping her brush her teeth and comb her hair. Thank god I had the forethought to bathe them last night. At least that was one thing I wouldn't have to deal with this morning.

"Are you okay to get dressed by yourself? The clothes you picked out last night are folded on your chair," I said.

I hurried out of the washroom, now focusing my attention on finding Jeremy. Where had he gone? I couldn't hear him anymore, and that was never a good sign.

"Jeremy?" I checked his bedroom; it was empty.

"Jeremy?" I checked the kitchen, it was empty.

I headed into the living room. "Jere—"

"Yes, daddy?" Jeremy cut me off as I was calling for him. He had emerged from under the coffee table. What he was doing there, I'll never know.

I finally managed to have both kids seated at the table, and fed them a delicious breakfast of pancakes and sausages. They didn't seem to mind that the pancakes were of the frozen variety, and that I had nuked the sausages in the microwave.

As they were nearing their last bite, I glanced at the clock. We were only running ten minutes late. So far this week, this has been our best time.

I quickly swallowed two pancakes and stuffed three sausages in my mouth. There was no time to sit down and eat when I had to take care of two kids by myself.

"Daddy, I can't find my shoes," Alia said.

"How about you wear your rain boots today?" I asked.

"But daddy, it's not raining."

"It's okay. You'll be well prepared." As I helped her put on her rain boots, I spotted Jeremy emptying his backpack onto the floor.

"Jeremy, buddy, what are you doing?" I asked.

"I can't find Captain Spaceman. He's gone."

I quickly scanned the living room, but his toy was nowhere to be found. I ran up to his room to look for it, but it wasn't there either. By the time I ran back down the stairs, I was out of breath.

"Captain Spaceman said he wants to stay

home today," I said to Jeremy as I stepped off the last step.

"But I need to talk to him. I need him." His voice was getting agitated. I knew that if I didn't nip this in the bud, he'd be crying all the way to daycare.

I handed him my phone, right after locking the screen. "Captain Spaceman said you can call him. You better call him now; he said he has a secret to tell you."

Jeremy ripped the phone out of my hands and pressed a random combination of numbers. I silently prayed that he wouldn't unlock my phone by accident. Last time, it had cost me an extra $19.32 on my phone bill for a call he had made to Indonesia.

As he started his conversation with Captain Spaceman, I turned around to find Alia with bare feet. She had taken off her rain boots.

"Alia, where are your boots?" I asked her.

"It's not raining, daddy. I need to find my shoes."

Resigned, I helped her look around the house for her shoes. After eight minutes of searching, I found them under her brother's bed.

I helped her put on her shoes, made sure they both had their backpacks on, and headed out the door. I was thanking my lucky stars that the daycare was providing them with lunch today; I don't even want to imagine how late we would have been if I had to pack their lunches on top of everything else.

As we walked to the subway station, Jeremy was still having his conversation with Captain Spaceman. I was holding onto both of their hands, walking as fast as their little legs would let them.

When we arrived at the station, I paid our fares and we waited for the subway to arrive. As the train pulled into the station, I glanced down at my watch. Less than an hour late. We were making progress.

Victoria Park

Locking the door behind me as I left my apartment, I grabbed my phone from my purse. While getting ready, I had received a text. It was from my best friend Kim.

> Kim: Where are you????
> Chelsea: Leaving now. Headed to Vic Park station. Meet me there?
> Kim: Too far. I thought we were meeting at Matt's?
> Chelsea: Come on. It's not that far. I'll wait for you.
> Kim: Fine
> Chelsea: See you

I was so focused on my phone that I almost bumped into someone on the street. I put my phone to sleep and placed it back in my purse.

Yesterday night, Kim and I decided that we would run for student council. I would be the president, and she would be the vice-president. School elections weren't really a competition, considering the students who actually chose to run. We were pretty much a shoe in.

We were supposed to head over to Matt's house, Kim's boyfriend, so that he could give us a ride to school. At the last moment, I decided to take the subway. The last few times he drove us, we were late because his car took forever to start. I didn't want to be late today.

As I was walking, I spotted a coffee shop, one of those little mom-and-pop-shop operations. I grabbed two lattes with skim milk, slipped a cardboard sleeve on both cups, and continued on my way to the station.

I heard my phone alerting me to a new message received. I didn't have any free hands, so I placed my drinks on top of a newspaper dispenser and retrieved my phone.

Kim: Why do we even need to go to school early???? Who cares?
Chelsea: We need to make a good impression, show that we care.
Kim: Ugh
Chelsea: You suck as VP
Kim: Thanks prez

Chelsea: Don't be late, ok? I'm almost there.

Kim: What if I am?

Chelsea: I'll dump your latte on the ground.

Kim: Ooooooooh. Big deal.

Chelsea: I'll add full-fat milk to it.

Kim: No! Anything but that, lol.

Chelsea: Just hurry

Kim: Relax. See you soon.

I really hoped Kim would get to the station quickly. I wanted us to get to school early and be the first ones to submit our bid for elections. Even though I was 99% sure we were a shoe in to win, I didn't want to take any chances. I wanted to be prepared.

As I continued walking, my feet started to hurt. Maybe wearing heels wasn't such a good idea, especially when I had to walk all the way to the station. I could feel blisters forming on the back of my heel.

Pushing the pain aside, I started daydreaming. Being president of the school would be amazing. At our school, being president was mostly just a title. The president didn't have any clout or say in anything that went on at school. All they did was play messenger between the school administration and the students.

I really hoped that we would be able to pull it off. Not only would being school president look impressive on my university applications, but it actually didn't seem to involve that much work.

I could see the station now, and quickened my pace subconsciously. I immediately returned to my original pace, after the shooting pain in my feet reminded me why I had slowed down in the first place.

I couldn't believe my eyes. Standing in front of the station doors was Kim.

"How did you get here so fast? I honestly thought I'd be waiting for you for at least fifteen minutes. Maybe this vice-president thing will change you, after all," I said.

"Yeah, don't count on it," said a familiar voice. I turned around to see Matt walking towards us. He was smoking a cigarette, and threw it to the ground as he approached.

"Ah," I said. "I should have known. Of course, you got a ride. Lame."

"Me, lame? No," she said in mock shock.

"I'll see you later, babe. Gotta go pick up Ryan

and Steven," Matt said. He gave her a goodbye kiss before leaving.

"Wow, you have him whipped. I can't believe he drove you to the station when the school is literally five minutes away from his house," I said.

"Yeah, I know," she replied, laughing my comment away.

We both went into the station and waited for the train to arrive.

Main Street

I didn't know where I was. I just woke up in a strange apartment, with a stranger I didn't know. I didn't remember anything that happened last night, but my raging headache gave me a few clues.

I looked at the man lying in bed beside me. He had shoulder length hair dyed green, a nose piercing, an eyebrow piercing, and six different loops coming out of his ears. I have to say, he's not usually the type I go for.

I slowly got out of bed and looked for my clothes. I found my boxers lying on the floor at the foot of the bed. My jeans had found their way under the bed, and my shirt had entangled itself in the sheets.

As I put on my clothes, I stared at the man lying down in the bed. I tried to think of what his name was, but nothing came to mind. I couldn't believe that I had woken up in a stranger's bed. I never thought I'd be a one-night-stand kind of guy.

I debated whether or not I should wake him up. I wanted to leave as soon as possible, especially considering I had no idea where I was. On the other hand, I didn't want to be rude and just disappear while he slept.

I sat down on the bed, and decided to wake him up. I gently nudged his shoulder. When that didn't do anything, I shook him a bit harder.

"Yeah?" he asked, as he rubbed sleep out of his eyes.

"Uh, hi," I said. I didn't know what else to say.

He slowly rose out of bed, until he was sitting right beside me. He ran his hands through his hair, and finally settled his gaze on me.

"Morning. How did you sleep?" he asked me.

"Not sure. Woke up with a killer headache."

He was quiet. Then he said, "Sorry, I don't have any pain killers."

We both remained quiet, and nothing more was said. After a few minutes of awkward silence, he got up and walked over to his bedroom door. He was completely naked.

"Did you want to take a shower?" he asked, as he wrapped the towel that was hanging behind the door around his waist.

"Nah, it's okay. I should probably head home."

"Yeah, I've got work in a few hours."

"Yeah, okay," I said. "I guess I should probably get going."

"Okay, see you."

I walked to the door, swung it open, and waved bye before leaving. As the door closed behind me, I could hear the click of the lock.

After walking through the hallway and going down three flights of stairs, I found my way outside. I looked around, but didn't recognize anything. I don't think I've ever been in this part of Toronto before.

I figured if I walked straight in any one direction, I would eventually find a subway station. I decided to turn right and started walking in that direction.

I still couldn't believe what had happened. I wasn't the type of guy who just hooked up with random people. There had to be a connection, a future of some sort (even if that future would prove to be short). I didn't understand how I ended up in this situation.

I tried to think back to last night. What had happened? I remember meeting my friends at a bar, and then going down to Church Street to hit up a few clubs. I drank a lot, but I've also drank a lot in the past whenever we went out. Usually the worst that happened to me was waking up passed out on my friend's living room couch.

I didn't remember meeting anyone there, but clearly I must have. I couldn't even remember his name. *Oh, great*, I thought to myself, *I didn't even think to ask his name before leaving.*

I continued pondering it all as I was looking for a subway station. After a few more minutes of walking, I finally spotted a station. Relief swept over me. I couldn't wait to get back home.

As I walked into the subway station, I silently hoped that my wallet would be in my pocket. I had forgotten to check before leaving that guy's place. I placed my hand in my back pocket, and...relief swept over me; I pulled out my wallet.

After paying my fare, I headed down to the platform, and waited for the train to arrive. As the train pulled into the station, all I could think about was going back home and cozying up on the couch with a blanket.

Woodbine

There's no more milk. I need to get milk. I need somewhere to write it down, but I can't find any paper lying around. Where did all my paper go?

Check the kitchen drawer. I put some paper in there. There's a pen near the phone.

The voice was always there, but at least I was in control today. She always stayed with me, and did things I didn't know about. The voice tended to get me in trouble. I didn't want to get in trouble today.

I don't get you in trouble. I'm just trying to help you. Why haven't you moved? Go get the paper. We need a grocery list.

Yes, a grocery list is a good idea. We're running out of a lot of things. Vivian, our caretaker, only comes over once a week now. They won't pay for any more visits, but we can get along just fine without her.

Vivian thinks that I'm crazy, but she's nice about it. I don't mind, but the voice hates it. She always—

She belittles me, and treats me like I am a figment of your imagination. At least she's better than Courtney. What a character.

"Courtney wasn't being mean. She thought the medication would help me. She even said that I might be able to get a job. We would make our own money," I said to the voice.

No, you would make your own money. The medication would make me go away. She wanted to get rid of me, and you were going to let her.

"No, no. I wasn't. I was going to pretend. I was going to get a job, and then I would stop taking the medication. Remember, I told you before. You need to clean your ears."

All of a sudden, I burst into a fit of laughter. I couldn't stop laughing. Of course, the voice couldn't clean her ears. Her ears were my ears.

I grabbed the piece of paper from the drawer and found the pencil near the phone.

"What do we need, what do we need? Milk. And bread. And honey!"

You don't even like honey.

Oh yeah, I forgot. I wrote down milk and bread.

You wrote it wrong. It's b-r-e-a-d.

Oops, I forgot the *a*. I squeezed in an *a* between the *e* and *d*.

Don't forget chips. And ice cream. Add chocolate milk.

I added everything the voice said to the list. I couldn't think of anything else to add, so I folded the list and put it in my pocket.

"It's time to go to the store now."

Shh. Remember, you can't talk out loud when we go outside. They'll give you medication again, and I'll go away. Do you want me to go away?

No. I don't want the voice to go anywhere. I don't want you to go anywhere. Stay!

I put on my jacket, the green one with a big number seven on it. I was still wearing my pajama pants, but it's okay, I can wear them outside. I took my debit card and two subway tokens from the desk in the living room, and put them in my pocket.

Do you remember the PIN? Don't forget your PIN like last time. Do you want a hint? I can give you a hint.

I don't need a hint. Vivian helped me change my PIN. She said to pick something I would never forget. I chose something easy, that I would never forget: the year I started hearing the voice.

I closed the door behind me, and walked to the elevator.

You forgot to lock the door. The door, the door, the door! We'll get robbed, and nasty Vivian will make me go away. The door, the door! You need to lock the door!

I yelled out, "Shut up, I know!" I realized I wasn't supposed to talk in public. "Sorry," I whispered.

I went back to the door and locked it. I tried twisting the knob, just to make sure. Good, it was locked.

I went back to the elevator, and waited patiently as it came. When it came, I went down to the lobby and walked into the street. The voice stayed quiet, and didn't say anything. Not even when we passed a baby. The voice really liked babies, because they made funny faces and didn't judge us.

We're almost there, we're almost there.

I could see the subway station, and I walked faster. I was so excited to go grocery shopping. Vivian would be proud of me.

When we got to the subway station, I forgot what I had to do with my token.

Put it in the box. That one.

The voice looked at a see-through box on the counter, right beside the collector's booth. Oh yes, I remembered now. I put my token in and walked to the subway platform.

When the subway came into the station, people pushed me as I tried to get in. I wanted to push them back. I hated when people touched me.

Don't, they'll take me away. Don't fight them, please.

I didn't want to lose the voice. I decided to sit down and stay quiet until we arrived at the grocery store.

Coxwell

"Hurry up, we need to leave," Georgina said.

I quickly grabbed my bag and followed her out the door. There was no point in talking back. She would always win.

"Damn it, Britney, where's my scarf?" she rudely asked.

"Um, I think you left it inside," I said. "Do you want me to go get it for you?"

"Well, it's damn well not going to get itself."

I quickly unlocked the door and retrieved her scarf. When I handed it to her, she took it without saying anything.

Georgina and I were roommates. We had signed a lease for one year, and we were only into the third month. At first I didn't think it would be that big of a deal, mixing my work and personal life, but I was soon proven wrong. I regretted extending my offer of friendship to her, in addition to my offer of being her roommate when she needed someone to split the bills with.

As we started walking towards the subway station, I was hoping that she would remain quiet for the entire walk. Of course, being me, I had no such luck.

"There are so many damn Chinese around," she huffed.

"That's kind of racist," I told her. She ignored me and continued her list of complaints.

She pointed out two kids walking on the sidewalk. "Where are their parents? What are they doing, gallivanting around? They're probably up to no good."

I sighed. "They're probably on their way to school. They have backpacks on."

"Yeah, their backpacks are probably full of drugs. Look at that black one." She pointed to a boy who couldn't have been older than 12. "He's probably a drug dealer. They're always blacks."

"He's just a kid, on his way to school." I thought about saying more, but realized there was no point. Nothing would stop her tirade.

When we arrived at a crosswalk, she took out a cigarette and lit it up.

"Would you mind not smoking while we're walking together?" I asked her. We had previously had discussions in regards to her smoking around me, and she was aware of my sensitivity to smoke.

"Buck up. It's not going to kill you," she said between puffs.

"Um, actually, yeah it will. Cancer? You know..." I stopped trying to reason with her, and decided to walk ahead of her to avoid the smoke.

"You damn baby. Grow a spine," she growled at me. She threw her cigarette on the floor and matched my pace so we were once more walking side by side.

"Look at that damn delinquent," she said, as she pointed out a man skateboarding on the sidewalk.

This time, I chose to remain silent. I thought that maybe, just maybe, she would stop talking if I stopped responding. Yet again, I had no such luck.

"This country is going to shambles. All these damn miscreants." I didn't know who she was talking about specifically, but with her, it didn't really matter.

We continued walking, and I internally rejoiced when I spotted the subway station. As we walked inside, I removed my Metropass from my purse. I swiped it and went through the automatic turnstile.

"Damn rotten no good...I want to speak to

your manager!" I heard Georgina shouting from behind me. She was at the collector's booth, and was having an argument with the collector.

I walked over to the collector's booth. "Georgina, what's going on?" It was most likely something ridiculous, but I asked anyways.

"This damn imbecile won't answer a simple question!" she bellowed.

I wanted to ask her what the question was, but I knew that it was going to be fruitless.

"Ma'am, please pay your fare and enter the station, or I will call security who will escort you off the premises," said the collector.

"Georgina, come on," I pleaded with her. "We're going to be late for work."

"Not until this damned imbecile tells me why there are so many damn imbeciles working in this place," she replied.

"Please, Georgina..."

"Fine, fine. Quit your yapping." She flashed her Metropass and passed through the turnstile, but not before giving the collector the finger.

We went down to the platform and waited for the train to arrive. As the train pulled into the station, I silently prayed that she would keep her mouth shut for the duration of the ride.

Greenwood

When I woke up this morning, Geneviève was nowhere to be found. I rolled out of bed, feeling more tired than when I went to sleep last night. Assuming she probably went out for a run, I jumped into the shower.

The warm jets of water hitting my body made me crave the warmth and comfort of our bed. I wish I didn't have to go to work today. I wish I could just stay home all day, cuddling in bed with Geneviève, watching movies.

Stepping out of the shower, I wrapped a towel around myself. I looked at my reflection in the mirror, pleased with what I saw. It had taken a long time to get to this point, but I was finally happy with being just plain old me.

I went into my closet and picked out a pair of faded jeans; my lucky pair. I grabbed a t-shirt from my dresser and rushed downstairs whilst in the middle of putting it on.

When I arrived at the base of the stairs, I could smell something delicious coming from the kitchen. Following my nose, I discovered a dining table full of breakfast goodies: pancakes, eggs, bacon, sausages, oranges, strawberries, hash browns, and toasts. My stomach rumbled in anticipation of this delightful breakfast.

"Geneviève?" I called out for her, but I received no answer in response. As hungry as I was, I wanted to thank her first for the wonderful surprise.

I searched the entire house, but I couldn't find her. If she had gone out for a run, she should be back by now. I tried calling her cell phone, but there was no answer.

I went back into the kitchen and sat at the table. As I was about to grab a piece of bacon to nibble on until I found her, I spotted an envelope that had been placed in my plate.

I picked up the envelope and examined it. My name was written in Geneviève's beautiful cursive. I opened the envelope and found a letter inside.

To my sweet Madison,

I cannot begin to express to you the joy you have brought into my life. Every day is a wonderful adventure, because you are part of it.

I want you to know that I love you with all my heart. I will stand strongly by your side. I will love you and care for you until my dying breath. Je t'aime.

With all the love contained within this little heart of mine,
Geneviève XOXO

I read the letter over again, holding my hand to my heart. The letter was so touching, so moving. In that moment, all I wanted to do was find Geneviève, kiss her, and tell her that I love her.

"I love you," a voice behind me said. As if my prayers were silently answered, Geneviève stood in the opening of the kitchen.

I quickly got out of my chair and ran into her arms. As we caressed, I could feel the beating of her heart falling into symphony with mine.

"Madison, I love you," she said.

"I love you too." I kissed her.

She put her hand in her pocket, but kept her fist tightly clenched when it came out. I couldn't make out what she was holding.

"Madison," she said as she stared deeply into my eyes. "Will you marry me?" She opened up her hand, and a beautiful ring was displayed in her palm.

"Yes! Yes, of course, yes. Yes!"

She placed the ring on my finger and kissed me passionately. I couldn't believe it. The love of my life just proposed to me. I was filled with so much joy.

We embraced for a while longer, and eventually made our way to the dining table. We ate breakfast in pure bliss, enveloped in happiness.

After we finished breakfast, I noticed the time and realized I had to leave for work. "Honey, I have to go to work. I'll miss you. I'll think about you every moment."

"I wish you didn't have to go now," she said, wrapping her hands around my waist.

"I know, I know. Me too. I'll be home soon."

"Okay. I can't wait to see you after work."

"I can't wait to show off this ring." I put my hand up, admiring the beautiful ring on my finger.

"I'll miss you," she said as she kissed me.

"I'll miss you too. I love you."

We continued saying "I love you" for about seven rounds, until I finally left the house and walked to the subway station.

While waiting for the train to arrive, I couldn't help but daydream about her, about my beautiful Geneviève. When the train pulled into the station, I stepped inside feeling on top of the world.

Donlands

I was washing myself in the tub, but I didn't turn the water on. I didn't want Uncle to wake up, so I was as quiet as I could be. I put water in a bucket, and then lathered soap all over my body. I wasn't able to wash pass my stomach, because my arms still hurt from yesterday.

I quickly rinsed myself off and covered up with a towel. I brushed my teeth and spit out into the sink. After I was done, I carefully emptied the bucket of water and placed it back under the sink.

The first thing I did when I got back to my room was lock the door. I had to do it slowly, because once the *click* of the lock woke up Uncle. He wasn't happy when he got woken up.

I quickly dried myself off and put on my school uniform. It was ugly and I hated it; at least I wasn't the only one forced to wear it. After I was dressed, I made sure all my homework and books were in my backpack.

I realized that I had left my math homework on the kitchen table last night. I had heard my Uncle coming home, and ran to hide in my room before he saw me. In that moment of panic, I forgot to take my things with me.

I slowly crept into the kitchen. The lights were turned off downstairs, so I was pretty sure he was sleeping. I didn't want to take any chance, so I tiptoed to the table and picked up my homework.

When I picked it up, it felt weird. It didn't feel like paper. I didn't want to risk turning on the lights, so I grabbed it and left the house. After making sure that I was out of sight from the house, I looked down at my homework.

In the light of day, I could see that my homework was completely ruined. The entire page was wrinkled, as if it had been wet and then dried. There was a red stain and a yellow stain covering the top of the page. There was a smear of something brown on all the answers I had written.

My homework was ruined. There was no way I could hand this in to Mr. Mackey. I would get a zero for yesterday's homework assignment.

As I walked to the subway station, I tried not to cry. A few tears escaped, but I was able to stop crying. I wiped my eyes, pretending that something flew in there. Now if anyone saw a tear on my face when they walked by, they would just assume it was caused by whatever flew into my eyes.

I tried to think of what I would say to Mr. Mackey. I knew he wouldn't believe me. And if I showed him my homework, he would just blame me for doing it. I had to think of a way to not get in trouble. I couldn't let him call Uncle.

The more I thought about ways to get out of trouble with Mr. Mackey, the more I got angry with Uncle. I hated Uncle. I hated him so much.

It wasn't fair that I had to live with him. My parents sent me here so I could go to a good school. They said I would be able to get into a good university without any problems, since all my transcripts would be Canadian. I don't care about any of that stuff. I didn't want to leave, but they made me. They made me come live here with my Uncle.

I told my parents the first time that Uncle hurt me. They told me that I was overreacting, and that I should be grateful that he even allowed me stay with him. After that day, I started hating them too.

I spotted a rock on the floor and I started kicking it. I imagined that it was Uncle's face. I kicked it hard, and it hit a car that was parked on the side of the street.

I kept on trying to think of what I would say

to Mr. Mackey. If I got to school early enough, maybe I could ask him for a new homework sheet. I hoped he would be in a good mood today. I was always quiet in class; I hoped he remembered that I was good.

As I arrived at the subway station, I took out my Metropass and student ID from my backpack. I showed my two cards to the man inside the booth, and went to wait at the subway platform.

When the subway arrived, I waited until everyone got in before getting on. I tried to think of happy thoughts. At least I would be at school for the day, and not at Uncle's.

Pape

The agony that I was feeling was tearing me apart. I couldn't go on like this any longer. There is no hope. Only despair. Only pain.

My mind was clouded; I couldn't think straight. I looked at the bottle of pills lying on the table. My mother's sleeping pills. I had stolen them the last time I saw her. The last time I would ever see her.

I played with the bottle in my hands, looking at the label. I opened the bottle, and looked at the little pills inside. It would be easy, so easy.

I placed the bottle back down on the table, forgetting to place the cap back on. I watched one pill fall to the floor. Then two. Then three. The rest remained in the bottle.

I grasped my head with my hands, pulling the skin on my face taut. Why was this so hard? Why was life full of misery? Why couldn't I just be happy?

I grabbed my notebook and pen from the table. Sometimes writing helped. Sometimes I was able to let go of everything, to impregnate the pages with my pain. It would all go away, just long enough for me to breath.

I uncapped the pen and starred at the blank page before me. I couldn't find the words. I couldn't think of them. I couldn't express the agony I felt.

And then some words came to mind.

Despair,
Waiting to cease
Existence
Life
Pain

The good,
The bad,
It matters not

Death
Destruction
Birth of pain

I glanced at what I wrote. It meant nothing. I closed my notebook and placed it back on the table. There would be no writing therapy today.

I glanced at the clock. The time didn't matter; it was just a habit. I couldn't think. I couldn't concentrate. I couldn't feel anything but pain.

The agony that kept me company, day in and day out, wouldn't let me rest. I couldn't sleep. I couldn't eat. I couldn't function.

I needed to stop the pain. I needed to clear my mind. I tried to think of a way to do it, but I couldn't concentrate. I just wanted all the noise to stop.

I couldn't stay here anymore. I felt as if the walls were closing in on me. I had to get out, I had to leave.

I left my apartment and walked outside. I thought the fresh air might help, but it didn't. Everyone was walking about, acting as if nothing was wrong. How could they pretend that everything was fine, while I was dying inside?

I watched the traffic, looking at the cars as they sped by. It would be so easy. Just one step. My ticket to freedom.

I stood on the curb for a while, watching cars go by. I thought about it, I really did. But I couldn't do it. Why couldn't I do it? Was I destined to live in this agony forever?

I continued walking until I saw a subway station. As soon as I saw it, I started walking in that direction. Maybe my answer was there.

In the station, I didn't know where I was going. I paid my fare with the change in my pocket, and went to wait at the bus terminal. I watched a few buses unload and load passengers, leaving quietly out of the station. Why was the station so quiet? Why couldn't the noise drown out the thoughts in my head?

I decided to go down to the subway platform. The trains are really loud when they come into the station. Maybe I would finally be able to think. Maybe I would be free.

On the platform, I was leaning against the wall, staring at the yellow line at the edge of the platform. I don't know what happened, but suddenly I was looking down at my feet which were on the yellow line. When did I move from the wall?

The agony kept on hovering over me, like a shadow. I looked down into the tunnel. There was garbage on the tracks. I saw a rat scurry; scurrying like the million thoughts in my head, not one of them pleasant.

It would be so easy. Just one more step. The darkness would come. I would be free.

My heart ached; it physically ached. My head was pounding, my heart was racing. How would I ever be able to live like this?

I brought my hands up to my face and took in a deep breath. From the corner of my eye, I saw a bright light signaling an incoming train. I looked at the light. It was so bright. There was no darkness there.

As the train pulled into the opening of the station, I closed my eyes. The agony. The pain. The despair. There was no hope.

Opening my eyes, I jumped onto the tracks.

Chester

"Mommy, wake up," I said as I tapped on my mommy's shoulder.

"What?...Oh, Jimmy...Go get ready for school, I'll be right up," my mommy said. She said it really low, almost like a whisper, but I had very good hearing.

I yelled out "Okay, mommy!" as I ran out of her bedroom. I went in my room and looked at my morning schedule. The first item was BRUSH YOUR TEETH.

In the bathroom, I put toothpaste on my toothbrush. Not a lot like mommy did. You're only supposed to put on a pea size amount; that's what my dentist said. I started brushing the front of my top teeth. I counted to 120, and then went to the back. After another 120, I started brushing the front of my bottom teeth. And then another 120 for the back of my bottom teeth.

I spit into the sink, and rinsed out my mouth. I put mouthwash in my blue bathroom cup, and counted to 30 as I swished the green liquid in my mouth.

The next item on my morning schedule was GET DRESSED. I took off my pajamas and put on the clothes mommy had set out for me the night before. Socks and underwear first. Then my pants and t-shirt. I slipped my feet into my sandals. I still didn't know how to tie shows with laces, and I hated Velcro shoes because of the noise it made.

I returned to my schedule. The next thing on my list was MAKE BED. I untangled my sheet and spread it on the bed. I spread my comforter on top of that, making sure it covered the pillows. Done.

The next thing on my list was EAT BREAKFAST. I ran downstairs to the kitchen, and saw mommy sitting at the table.

"Hey Jimmy. Do you want milk or orange juice today?" my mommy asked me.

"Orange juice!" I exclaimed.

My mommy poured my orange juice into a blue cup, and put milk into the blue bowl that held my cereal. I tried to eat my cereal slowly; mommy said I ate too fast and that was why my tummy was always upset.

"I'm finished, mommy," I said.

"What do you do now?" she asked.

"Um..." I knew this one, but I forgot it. Oh

yeah, I remembered now. "Put my dishes in the sink!"

"That's right. Good job, Jimmy." I loved it when I made mommy happy.

After I put my dishes in the sink, I ran back upstairs to look at my morning schedule. There was only one thing left, and I would be done. The last thing on the list was GET SCHOOLBAG. I grabbed my schoolbag from the floor and ran back downstairs.

"I'm ready mommy, I'm ready," I said.

"Alright. Let's get going, champ."

I followed my mommy outside, and watched as she locked the door. After she locked the door, I twisted it three times to make sure it was locked.

I held mommy's hand while we walked to the subway station. I started playing my games like I do every morning.

The first game I played was called *Rainbow Cars*. I would close my eyes and then open them. I would yell out the color of the first car I saw.

"Blue car!" I yelled out as a blue car drove by.

"Jimmy, don't close your eyes when you're walking outside. It's dangerous. Play *Chicken Chicken* instead," mommy said.

"Ok," I said.

I loved playing *Chicken Chicken*. 1 chicken, 2 chickens, 3 chickens. 2 chickens, 4 chickens, 6 chickens. 3 chickens, 6 chickens, 9 chickens. 4 chickens, 8 chickens, 12 chickens. 5 chickens, 10 chickens, 15 chickens.

The furthest I'd ever gotten in a game was '10 chickens, 20 chickens, 30 chickens'. After that, I couldn't remember what was next.

When we got to the subway station, mommy showed her subway card, and gave a ticket for me. I waved to the man behind the glass. "Hi, mister!"

The man waved back at me, and said "Hi."

When we were waiting for the subway to come, I had to hold mommy's hand. She said that the subway was fast and made a lot of wind, so I had to be careful. I held onto her hand tightly; I didn't want the subway to blow me away.

When the subway came into the station, I counted all the people that got off. 1, 2, 3, 4, 5, 6 and a half. One woman had a baby in her stomach, so she counted as one and a half.

I followed mommy into the subway and sat down beside her. Now I would get to play my favorite game, *Word Count*. I would count all the words in all the ads on the subway.

Broadview

"Have you accepted your Lord and Saviour, Jesus Christ? There is no time to wait. The rapture will soon be upon us. You must repent your sins immediately, and accept the light of the Lord into your life. He is the only one who can save you," I said to a couple that walked into the subway station.

Every morning, I stood outside a different subway station preaching about our good Lord. It was my duty to save as many people as possible. The end would soon be near, and God wanted me to help save his people.

The couple who I was preaching to ignored me as they walked into the station. That's fine. It didn't matter how people ignored the good Lord, so long as I could reach at least one person.

I handed out my flyer to people as they walked into the station. Most ignored me and I was left standing with my hand outreached, holding onto the flyer. Some would take it, but I saw them throw it out as soon as they walked into the station.

I saw a group of girls walking towards the station. What a perfect opportunity! They all looked like dirty whores, with their clothing and makeup. They needed saving.

"Accept the Lord into your lives, and rid yourselves of your sins. He can cleanse you, make you pure again. You don't have to walk the path of a harlot. Cover yourselves! The Lord expects modesty from all His children. It is not too late; you can save yourselves. Repent and accept the light of our Lord and Saviour," I preached to the group of girls.

I extended my flyer towards them, and all but one ignored me. The girl in the short skirt who took my flyer examined it. I was getting through to her.

"Young woman, do not allow yourself to be driven down the Devil's path. Secure your spot in heaven, ensuring that you are not left behind during the rapture. God loves all his children. God love you," I said to her.

The girl scrunched up my flyer into a ball and threw it at me. Her and her friends laughed as they walked into the station.

"That's alright, the Lord still loves you. You can still be saved!" I yelled after her.

Sometimes I got really discouraged. I knew that God wanted me to preach his message, to save his children. But people were so full of the Devil, that sometimes it seemed like a losing battle. I looked down at my flyer, reading it to remember my mission.

THE END IS NEAR! ARE YOU PREPARED?

The end of times is soon upon us! Will you be saved when the rapture comes?

Matthew 24:42 - Watch therefore: for ye know not what hour your Lord doth come.
There is still time to accept the Lord Jesus Christ into your souls. Let him cleanse you, make you reborn again.

The light of heaven shines brightly on those who repent their sins!

Revelation 20:4 - And I saw thrones, and they sat upon them, and judgment was given unto them: and [I saw] the souls of them that were beheaded for the witness of Jesus, and for the word of God, and which had not worshipped the beast, neither his image, neither had received [his] mark upon their foreheads, or in their hands; and they lived and reigned with Christ a thousand years.

Do not let the devil trick you! Your Father awaits you in heaven. Accept your Lord and Saviour today!

Reading over my flyer reenergized me. It was my sacred duty to spread His word. It was my duty to ensure that His children found their way home.

"Sir, have you accepted Jesus Christ as your Lord and Saviour? The end is near. There is no time to wait. Repent your sins today, and allow the love of the Lord to shine onto you," I said to a man coming out of the station.

A woman approached me from my left with a child. "Accept the Lord into your life. Let the light shine down on you, and eliminate the Devil's hold on your mind. Do not let yourself and your child be consumed by flames when the rapture comes," I preached.

The woman ignored me as she walked into the station. That's all right. I was just a messenger; I couldn't force her to see the light.

I handed out my flyer to a few more of God's children. One man read it and held onto it as he disappeared into the station. I had guided another child of His onto the path of light and redemption.

Castle Frank

I woke up to a putrid smell emanating from my room. I forced myself to get up, even though the warmth of my bed protested. I sat up in bed, and swung my legs onto the floor.

"Uh, what is that?" I said in surprise. I had stepped into something rather squishy. I looked down and saw my foot firmly planted in dog poop.

"Boomer, what the hell?" I looked at my dog Boomer, lying on my bed. "Why would you poop on the floor? I took you out last night!"

She looked at me with her big brown puppy-dog eyes as I started cleaning up her mess. I tried to hold in my breath while I scooped up her poop into a grocery bag. I cleaned the floor with some paper towels and soap, making sure I didn't miss a spot.

I put on my shoes, after cleaning my feet, and headed out into the hallway to dump the smelly evidence down into the garbage chute. On my way back to my apartment, a neighbour's door opened.

"Nice outfit," said my neighbour Clarisse, as she locked up her door. I had the biggest crush on her.

I looked down at what I was wearing: a pair of blue and white striped boxer, an old faded t-shirt, and a pair of shoes.

"Yeah, I..." I felt my cheeks flush. "I, uh...I had to throw something out." Thinking I hadn't explained myself adequately, I added, "Boomer had an accident."

"Ah, that's too bad."

"You look nice." She was wearing a pair of jeans and a navy blue sweater. To me, she looked nice in anything.

"Thanks. You do too, Mr. Boxer Boy." She laughed. What a beautiful laugh.

"Do you want to go grab some breakfast? On me?" I talked calmly, but my heart was beating fast against my chest.

"Sorry, Brian. I have to go to work." She looked genuinely apologetic.

"Oh, okay."

"Walk me to Castle Frank?"

My face lit up with joy. "Really? I mean, yeah, sure." I waited for her to lead the way.

All of a sudden, she burst into laughter. "Are you sure you don't want to change first?"

I looked down at my boxers. "Oh yeah. Give

me a moment.

I quickly ran into my apartment and changed into a pair of jeans and a t-shirt. I ran into the room and scooped Boomer off the bed; she hadn't moved at all.

"You're getting an early walk this morning," I said. I put on her leash and brought her out into the hallway with me. Clarisse liked Boomer. Maybe I'd score extra brownie points by taking her with us.

"Hey Boomer! You're so cute. Yes you are, yes you are. Who's a good doggy?" Clarisse had bent down to pet Boomer.

"Ready?" I asked.

"Let's go."

We left the apartment building, walking side by side. No one said anything, and the silence was getting to be a little awkward. I liked her so much, but I didn't want to blow it. I had to think of the right thing to say.

"So," I began, "the weather's nice, yeah?"

"Yeah, it's not bad."

"I was wondering if you would..." My words trailed off. I lost my nerve.

"Wondering what?"

"Wondering, um...I was wondering if you

would like to go out with me sometime." I just blurted it out. What was the worse she could say? No? Oh god, please don't let her say no.

As I saw her open her mouth to reply, all I could think was *please don't say no*. I wish I hadn't asked her at all. Now she would think I'm a creep, and she wouldn't want to hang out with me anymore.

"Thanks for asking," she said.

Oh great, I thought to myself, *here comes the letdown*.

She continued, "I would love to go out with you."

"Really? I mean, that's great. Tonight?" My cheeks were surely flushed now.

"Sure. I'll be home at five."

"Okay. I'll come knock on your door at five then."

We continued walking the rest of the way in silence. I kept on sneaking glances at her, and noticed her sneaking a few too.

When we arrived at the station, we said an awkward goodbye. I waited until I couldn't see her anymore, and then headed back home.

"I've got a date tonight, Boomer!"

Boomer looked up at me with indifference.

On the rest of my walk home, I couldn't help but beam with joy. 5:00 PM couldn't arrive soon enough.

Sherbourne

The minute I woke up, I felt like throwing up. I couldn't believe that today was the day. It seemed so far away just a week ago.

I picked up the phone and called my best friend Cynthia. "I can't do it. I can't."

"Pam, you can do it. You've been waiting for this day. I'll be right there supporting you. So will Alex and your parents," Cynthia said.

I started crying. "I can't. I can't. I don't want to see him. I can't."

"You can do it. We'll be right there for you. You need to do this for yourself."

"Okay." She was right, I needed to do this.

"I'll meet you at the subway station, okay? I'm here for you."

"Okay. Thanks Cynthia."

I hung up the phone, and stared blankly at my wall. I tried to force myself to get up, but my body wouldn't cooperate.

I was hoping this day would never come. How could I go in there and face him? How could I look at him, after what he had done to me?

After a few more moments of aimlessly staring in front of me, I found the strength within me to get up. I slowly showered, and got dressed.

Today, I would have to face the man who raped me. If I closed my eyes, I could remember it as if it happened yesterday.

I was at a club with my friends, and slipped away to go to the washroom. I didn't notice the man who followed me as I walked down the stairs. As I opened the door of the washroom, I was pushed into a stall with force. I...

I don't want to remember the rest.

I paced back and forth in my living room, trying to make sense of my thoughts. I didn't want to go. But I wanted to. My feelings didn't make any sense. I wanted to make him pay for what he did; but I didn't want to face him.

After a few more minutes of pacing, I somehow summoned the courage to leave the house. I locked the door, and walked slowly down my porch steps.

As I made my way to the subway station, a voice in my head kept on telling me that I was strong, that I could do it. There was also another voice telling me to go back home.

I concentrated on my steps, putting one foot in front of the other. Left. Right. Left Right. Maybe the monotony would help calm my mind.

It didn't work.

All I could think about was the way his hand felt against my body. Against my neck. Against my arms. Against my back. His hands were so cold.

I tried to shake the memory from my head. I needed to find something else to concentrate on. Anything else would suffice.

I saw two children running in front of their parents, playing with a basketball. A girl and a boy. The boy was wearing a red t-shirt. Red...

Red just like the letter emblazoned on his baseball cap. I saw it when it fell on the floor, in the bathroom stall. I remember it so clearly. It was a green baseball cap with the letter P stitched in bright red.

All of a sudden, I felt like throwing up again. I wanted to run back home, to lock the door and never come out.

I just wanted all the pain to stop.

Before I knew it, I had arrived at the entrance to the subway station. Cynthia was waiting there for me, holding two cups of coffee.

"Hey Pam. How are you holding up?" she asked as she handed me a cup of coffee.

I took the cup she offered me. "Badly. Thanks for the coffee."

"I know it's scary and I know you just want to run and hide in a corner, but you need to do this. You'll regret it if you don't."

"I guess."

I took a sip of coffee and followed her into the subway station. I barely paid attention as she paid our fare, and directed me to the platform.

I snapped out of my reverie as I heard the train enter the station. I followed Cynthia and sat down beside her. As the train doors closed, all I could think about was the man who raped me.

Bloor-Yonge

"Don't you ever think of coming back here again! You hear me?" my mother yelled as her face turned various shades of red.

"As if I'd ever want to come back to this hellhole! I'm never coming back again!" I yelled back at her.

I was being kicked out of my mom's house, for the sixth time this year. Ever since she divorced my dad, every small little thing set her off. She'd eventually get so upset that she'd kick me out. I would stay at my dad until she cooled down, and we'd start the charade all over again.

"You're just like him," my mom said.

"Yeah? Good. I rather be like him than like you."

I went into my room and slammed the door shut behind me, locking it. I grabbed my duffel bag from my closet, which was still partially packed from the last time she had kicked me out.

"You better open this damn door! This is my house! Open the door!" She was pounding on my bedroom door.

"I'm just trying to pack my things in peace and quiet! I don't need a lunatic screaming at me while I do it!"

I slipped a few things in my bag, including my computer and wallet, and zipped it up. I was done packing, but I kept the door locked just to drive her insane.

"Emery Russell Smith! You open that door right now!" I couldn't see her, but I could tell by her voice that her face must have been bright red by now. It always got that way when she yelled at me.

I took a deep breath and opened the door. "You're a lunatic! No wonder dad left!"

I expected her to yell back, but she fell silent instead. I knew that was a low blow. In the heat of the moment, I really didn't care how much I hurt her. But now I was starting to regret what I had said.

"Look, I'm sorry ma. I shouldn't have said that." I tried to give her a hug, but she swatted me away.

"Get out. Get out right now. I don't ever want to see you again." She wasn't yelling anymore. Her tone was eerily calm.

I sighed as I slung my duffel bag over my shoulder. I walked out the door, shouting out "I love you, ma!"

I heard the door slam behind me, and the distinctive sound of the door being locked. I quickly left my mom's condo and called my dad. I had to call three times before he finally picked up.

"Hey dad. Mom kicked me out again. Can you come pick me up?" I asked.

"Hey Em. Now's actually not a good time. I'm still at the office. I won't be back home until late tonight."

"I thought you were going to stop working long hours?"

"Yeah, yeah. Can you just take a cab or the subway? Gladys will be home; she'll let you in."

Gladys was my dad's new girlfriend. It was pretty convenient how they moved in together four months after my parents' divorce.

"Um, yeah. Sure, dad. I guess I'll see you tonight?" I asked.

"I'll be home late. Don't wait up."

As I was about to say "Bye", I heard the dial tone. He didn't even bother saying goodbye.

I angrily shoved my phone in my pocket and walked towards the subway station. I really wasn't looking forward to spending the week at my dad's. I hoped my mom would cool down soon so I could go back home.

As the subway rolled into the station, I clutched my phone. I wanted to call my mom, but there was no signal underground. Squished in between two others on the subway, I closed my eyes. I prayed my mom would let me come home soon.

Bay

I woke up early this morning, falling into my old routine subconsciously. As of yesterday, there was no longer a need for me to follow a routine. Why would I need to wake up early, if I no longer had a job to go to?

I still couldn't get over the shock of not having a job. Just yesterday, my supervisor called me into her office. She said it wasn't personal, that the company was cutting costs. They were laying people off, and I happened to be one of the casualties.

The thing that rubbed me the wrong way was this: why was I the one let go, when I had seniority over everyone else in my department? The more that I reflected on it, the more that I was convinced that it was indeed personal.

I didn't want to just stay home; I would drive myself crazy. I decided to go out for a walk, maybe do some grocery shopping. I quickly got dressed and headed out my apartment.

Outside, the air felt different. I felt as if everyone could tell that I'd just been fired, that everyone could see my pain. Holding my head up high, I started walking.

After wandering around for the better part of an hour, I found myself in front of Bay Station. I went into the station, paid my fare, and wandered around. There's not really anywhere to go, so I sat down on a bench.

In the quiet loudness of the station, I was able to drown out my thoughts. As I decided to get up and take the train to the grocery store, someone sat down beside me.

"Good day," said a man in a worn out grey wool sweater, and blue jeans.

"Good morning," I replied.

"Waiting for someone?"

"No. I'm just, uh...thinking."

He took out a pack of gum from his pocket. "Would you like a piece?"

"No, thank you."

We remained silent for few moments. I was usually a talkative person, but I wasn't into it today. Not wanting to be rude, I forced myself to interact with the man.

"Are you headed to work?" I asked. As the word *work* came out of my mouth, I silently cringed.

"No, no. Haven't worked in a long time.

People aren't too keen on hiring the homeless."

"Oh." I didn't know what else to say.

He didn't look homeless. I mean, yes, his clothes were a bit worn out, but they weren't dirty. He dressed better than a lot of people I worked with. Used to work with.

The man's laughter broke the silence. "It's okay; you don't have to be awkward about the fact that I'm homeless. It's not a bad word."

"Sorry, I didn't mean to..." I was searching my mind for what I should say.

"Don't worry about it. Name's Maurice." He extended his hand towards me.

"Scott." I shook his hand.

"Why do you look so glum, Scott?"

I didn't know what it was, but something made me want to open up to him. "I just lost my job. I was laid off yesterday. Just feeling kind of...I guess I'm just feeling mostly lost."

Maurice got up. "Come on, Scott. Let me buy you a cup of coffee."

I was taken aback. A homeless man, a man who barely had anything, was offering to buy me a cup of coffee.

"Thank you," I said. "I appreciate the offer,

but it's okay."

"Nonsense. Just because I'm homeless doesn't mean I can't afford to buy you a cup of coffee. There's a nice place, two stations down. Come on." He started walking towards the stairs leading down into the subway platform.

I got up and followed him. Here was a man who barely had anything, but was offering to buy me a cup of coffee to cheer me up.

When the train pulled into the station and we got onboard, we sat adjacent to each other. As the doors closed, I was thinking about how I could repay the favor to the kind man sitting beside me, who offered me a friendly cup of coffee.

St. George

I couldn't believe it. I was actually going to go to school by myself. My parents finally agreed to let me take the subway, as long as I go with my friend Vince. I was so excited. Up until today, I was the only one of my friends that still got driven to school by my parents.

I usually take a long time to get ready in the morning. Today, I couldn't get ready fast enough. I quickly put on my clothes and grabbed my backpack. I didn't take a shower, but mom and dad were getting my little sister Anna ready for school, so they didn't have time to notice.

I ran down the stairs and into the kitchen. I grabbed the lunch mom had packed me and put it in my bag. I grabbed a few slices of bacon from the pan on the stove, and ran to the front door.

"Bye mom! Bye dad! Bye Anna! See you later!" I shouted as the door slammed behind me.

I didn't want to take any chances that my parents would change their mind. I knew that they'd be upset with me that I didn't go hug them goodbye before leaving, but that's okay. They wouldn't be mad for long.

I tried walking at a normal pace, but I kept on breaking into a slow jog. I was so excited to finally be taking the subway by myself. Well, I would be taking it with Vince, but it's still the same thing. I would have no parents supervising me.

Yesterday, Vince told me to meet him at his house. He only lives five minutes away. By the time I got to his front door, I was out of breath. I just realized that I had been jogging the entire way.

I knocked on the door. Before I could knock a second time, the door swung open. It was Mrs. Klein, Vince's mom.

"Oh, look at you! You must be so excited. Your mother told me today would be the first time you're taking the subway to school." She gave me a hug, and squealed in my ears.

My cheeks were turning red from embarrassment, but Vince ran outside before she could continue.

"Bye, mom," Vince said. He hugged her and gave her a kiss on the cheek.

"Bye, Mrs. Klein," I said.

"Goodbye, boys. Get to school safely," she cooed after us.

Vince waited until we were out of sight from his home before he started talking. "Want to come hang out with me and James?"

"Yeah!" I said excitedly. James was one of the coolest kids in school.

"Okay. Did your parents give you any money?"

"No. I mean, I have the emergency money they gave me. Twenty dollars. But I'm not allowed to spend it unless it's an emergency."

"Don't worry. Just tell them you lost it."

I was a little uneasy about what Vince was asking me to do. Thinking back to the conversation, I started feeling uneasy about the entire thing. Since when did Vince hang out with James? Why wouldn't he have told me? I thought I was his best friend.

"When are we going to hang out with James? After school today? If so, I have to call my parents to ask them," I said.

"No," Vince said. "We're going to hang out right now. We're meeting up with him at the mall."

"But, we have school. We'll be late."

"Yeah, Einstein. We're skipping."

"But…" I realized I had no choice but to follow him. I didn't know how to get to school on my own, and I didn't want to call my parents. If they found out, they would never let me go to school alone again.

I followed him into the subway station, and gave my student ticket to the person sitting in the collector's booth. He didn't take it, but motioned to me to put it in the box on the counter, and I did. We then went to the platform to wait for the train.

When the train arrived, I followed Vince, even though I didn't want to. I wanted to go to school. As the doors closed, I made a wish: I hoped my parents would never find out about this.

www.ingramcontent.com/pod-product-compliance
Lightning Source LLC
Chambersburg PA
CBHW020639130626
46552CB00003B/1305